THE CAVE
CHALLENGE

BEAR GRYLLS
ADVENTURES

The Cave Challenge

BEAR GRYLLS
ILLUSTRATED BY EMMA McCANN

Bear Grylls

This edition published in Great Britain in 2019 by

4th Floor, Victoria House, Bloomsbury Square
London WC1B 4DA

A CIP catalogue record for this book
is available from the British Library.

ISBN: 978-1-786-96055-9
Also available as an ebook and in audio

11

Typeset in OpenDyslexia
Printed and bound in Great Britain
by Clays Ltd, Elcograf S.p.A.

Bear Grylls is an imprint of Bonnier Books UK,
owned by Bonnier Books
Sveavägen 56, Stockholm, Sweden

www.bonnierbooks.co.uk

To the young survivor
reading this book for the first time.
May your eyes always be wide open
to adventure, and your heart full
of courage and determination to
see your dreams through.

1

THE MILLION-DOLLAR QUESTION

Harry slunk along the path towards the clearing, feeling cross.

He'd just come from Construction Challenge, where everyone had been building a cart from bits of old junk. The wheels had been stiff, so Evie had squirted oil onto them ... and onto Harry's leg.

His jeans were *ruined*.

Harry bitterly ran through the list
of Bad Things That Had Happened
that day. First, he had spilled mayo on
his Chimp Skinny jeans. He loved his
Chimp Skinnys, they'd been brand new.
He was really upset with himself for
not being more careful. He'd washed
them as best he could, and missed out
on eating his lunch with the others.

2

Harry had changed into a spare
pair of jeans before Construction
Challenge. They weren't Chimps,
only Fully Leaded, but they still
looked pretty good.

But Evie had got oil on them!

He'd never be able to wash that
off.

Harry hardly dared to look at the
damage, but he guessed he had to.
He had to know how bad it really was.

The oil stain was thick and black,
right across one leg.

Harry always avoided getting dirty,
and took extra care of his clothes
and appearance. It was a calamity.

No one else at Camp cared. Well, Evie had given him some stupid compass to try to make up for the oil. She seemed to think there was something special about it, but it was just a compass. It wasn't going to make up for a ruined pair of jeans.

So Harry was heading back to change clothes *again*.

The next activity was Team Frisbee. Harry had deliberately chosen it because it was indoors, so he could wear his new white trainers and white Croc Byte T-shirt.

Harry had planned all his outfits at home in front of the mirror. This one made him look like his favourite basketball player.

4

"Hey, Harry!"

Harry heard his name being called, but he didn't feel like talking to anyone right now. He wasn't in the mood. He kept walking.

"Harry! Wait up!"

Harry sighed and turned round.

"Hi, guys."

"Harry, where are you going?"

Charlie and Joe fell in on either side of Harry, smiling and happy.

"I was just going to get changed for Team Frisbee," Harry said.

"Great – we're heading to the tent too," said Joe.

"Hey, have you read about this guy who didn't realise he'd won a million dollars?" Charlie said. "Can you imagine it? He didn't realise! What would you do if you accidentally won a million dollars?"

Before Harry could say anything,
Joe interrupted.

"I'd invent this thing like a global
map, right? And it would always tell
you exactly where you were, and how
to get to where you want to be."

Harry had to smile. Joe's total lack
of sense of direction was legendary.

"Don't we already have that?"
Harry said grumpily. "It's ... well.
It's satnav. Satellite navigation. It's
already been invented."

"Yeah, but mine would know every
single path and track and everything.
And ... wait for it! It would project
onto your eyes so you literally knew
where you were, every single second."

"I'd use a million dollars to invent the most totally cool games ever," Charlie decided. "They'd be totally immersive and they'd interact with real things too, so that you could make anything be fun. Like, we could shoot each other with laser guns in the game, and hide behind that tree there in real life."

"Maybe you two could work together," Harry suggested. "Satnav ... games, it's all electronics."

The other two boys looked at each other thoughtfully.

"Charlie, do you want to put your games on my satnav?" Joe said.

"Nah," Charlie said scornfully.

"But if you want, I can invent
a satnav that plays games ..."

They carried on arguing, which
meant Harry got out of having to
answer the question.

*What would I do with one million
dollars?* he thought, looking at the
massive oil stain on his Fully Leaded
jeans. Easy. He'd invent a special
high-tech fabric that dirt could
never stick to.

Harry glanced at his watch. They
were going to be late if they didn't
shift it. And he still needed to get
changed.

"Guys, gotta go!"

FRISBEE FROLICS

Harry had timed his leap perfectly.
As the Frisbee curved through the
air into his hands, he felt a thrill of
satisfaction as his fingers closed
around the spinning plastic.

Half a second later his feet hit
the ground. *Splat!*

Harry had landed right in the middle

of a muddy puddle. Dirty water splashed onto his white socks and white trainers and light grey cargo shorts.

They were supposed to have played in the sports hall, where it was nice and dry and clean. That was why he had chosen Team Frisbee. But the hall had been accidentally double-booked and Team Frisbee had to go outside onto the football pitch.

The damp and muddy football pitch.

Harry stared at his feet in horror, too distracted to notice someone snatching the Frisbee from his hand.

"Hey!" he protested.

"Ha!" The girl grinned, and flung it on to another teammate.

This was Team Frisbee. You had to get the Frisbee into the other team's goal. You couldn't run with the Frisbee, you could only throw it.

The other rules were that you could jump and catch the Frisbee if it was flying or knock it out of the air with your hand or your body. And you could snatch it away from someone who had just caught it, as long as you did it within one second.

Which the girl on the other team had done.

"*Harry!*" George shouted in frustration. He had been in the perfect position for Harry to pass to him.

Now the Frisbee was soaring into the goal. The Yellow team cheered while the Red team groaned and stared at Harry.

The ref blew her whistle.

"End of quarter, time to swap over!" she called.

The teams had five players each, but there were more than ten people playing. So, they swapped in and out at the end of each quarter, to give everyone a go. It was Harry's turn to swap out.

Probably best, he thought bitterly. *Yet another activity ruined.*

He plonked himself down on a bench
and glared at his spattered trainers.

Harry watched glumly from the
bench as the next quarter started. He
checked his pockets to see if he had
anything to wipe the mud off. But all
he pulled out was the compass that
Evie had given him.

Huh?

That was weird. He was sure he had
left it in his jeans in the tent. He must
have been in such a rush that he'd
picked it up again without thinking.

Harry studied it again. He still didn't see what Evie thought was special about it. It was just a regular compass – dial, needle ... and five directions!

As if that wasn't strange enough, the needle started spinning round and round.

Harry stared. What was the point of a compass with five directions and a broken needle?

He shoved it back into his pocket. Some of his teammates who were waiting for their turn were messing about on the playground near to the pitch. It had an all-weather surface, so Harry guessed he could join in and not get his trainers any more muddy, at least.

Harry balanced on the rolling log for a while before moving on to the rope swing. He gripped the rope between his hands and knees and swung himself out into mid-air...

Out of nowhere, a wall of solid rock came zooming straight at him.

"Aargh!"

Harry landed so hard on the rock
that he let go of the rope. He turned
around and saw there was nothing
behind him. He was right on the edge
of a narrow stone ledge, above a lake
of blue water.

Harry waved his arms in circles,
trying to regain his balance until at
last he was standing up straight again.

He stared around him in amazement.

Camp had vanished. The football
pitch, the playground, his friends –
all gone.

He looked up. His ledge was almost
at the bottom of a giant stone pit.

The water was a few metres below him, so clear that Harry could easily see the rocky bed. As he stared a shoal of fish swam lazily beneath him.

The pit was roughly circular, about thirty metres wide and deep. Its stone sides were almost hidden behind curtains of vines and creepers.

He looked up. There was a vast overhang all around the top, so that even if Harry could climb up there, it would be impossible to climb out.

And it was *incredibly* hot and humid.

The ledge was only three or four metres long. Harry moved up and down it, looking everywhere for a way up or out.

But he soon saw there *was* no way out. He was stuck here.

"Hi, there!"

A man's voice echoed around the stone pit.

Harry's head whipped around.

3

CAVEMAN

The man stood on some rocks a few
metres away, just above water level.
He had come out of a cave that Harry
hadn't noticed at first. Harry had
thought it was just a crack in the
rock.

The man was wearing a red oversuit
and a battered helmet with a lamp on
the front. The outfit made Harry think

of miners, except that the man also had a rucksack slung onto his back.

"There's a way out," the man called, "but you need to come over here."

"How?" Harry asked in frustration. "I can't see any way down."

The man smiled and pointed at the wall of vegetation that covered the stone behind Harry.

"You can use one of those vines behind you to swing over." He held a thumb up. "Find one that's about as thick as my thumb, and that's green and alive, not brown and dead. It needs to be strong and flexible."

"Um – okay."

Harry started to feel through the vines at the end of the ledge nearest to the man.

Some of the vines were too thin for him to get a good grip on. Some looked fine but snapped when he tugged on them. Eventually he had one about the right thickness and gave it a tug to test it.

"How's this –" he started to call, and flinched as a load of leaves and bugs fell down on him from above. He flicked off the bugs, shook his head and ran his fingers through his hair. His hair that he spent ages on every morning.

"Are you okay, buddy?" the man called.

Harry glowered down at himself.
The debris had left dirty smudges
on his white T-shirt, and his hair was
probably full of disgusting stuff. Yuck.

"No," he muttered. Then, so the
man could hear him, "Fine, thanks."

"Great. And that vine looks like
a good one. Swing yourself over."

Harry nervously gripped the vine.
He had seen people swinging on vines
in movies, but never in real life. But
he knew he couldn't stay on this
ledge forever.

Besides, he told himself, if the vine
snapped then the worst that could
happen would be he fell into the lake.
At least it would be a soft landing.

Harry tightened his grip and swung himself out into space.

The rocky pit and the blue water blurred past his eyes. The man came shooting towards him on a collision course.

Harry had a vision of them both ending up in the water, but the man caught him just in time.

"Well done!" he said, smiling. "You can let go of the vine now, champ."

Harry and the man were standing together on the rocks. The entrance to the cave was a jagged, mostly vertical crack, a bit taller than the man.

"You did it!" the man said
cheerfully. "I'm Bear," he said,
putting his hand out.

"I'm Harry."

"Well, Harry, I'm going to guide
you out of here."

Harry looked around. "Where are we? It's so hot!"

"Well, up there on the surface, it's all jungle. We're in a cenote."

The word sounded like 'sin-o-tee'. Harry had never heard it before.

"What's one of those?"

"Sometimes you get a really big cave underground, very close to the surface. The roof is so thin that it collapses, and the cave becomes a pit, like this."

The man waved a hand at the entrance behind him. I got here because I've been exploring this network of caves."

"You said there's no other way out," said Harry.

The man nodded.

"We'll have to retrace my steps to find our way back to the surface. Are you ready for some real adventure?"

"Sure," Harry said immediately, with a relieved smile. He already knew he would be clueless in a place like this. He needed a guide more than anything, and Bear looked like a sound guy.

Bear grinned.

"Okay, I'd better kit you out." He looked Harry up and down with a smile. "What you've got on looks pretty smart."

"Yeah? It's Croc Byte," said Harry,
pleased Bear thought his gear
looked smart, despite the mud
and everything.

"But," said Bear, "I'm afraid it's
not going to help you much where
we're going." He swung his rucksack
down to the ground and started to
rummage through it.

Harry's smile froze as he took
in the state of Bear's oversuit for
the first time.

"Uh – will it be dirty?" he asked.

"Filthy!" Bear smiled. "Mud and
slime everywhere. Are you okay
with that?"

Harry scowled. What could he
say? *No thanks, I'll just sit here
until someone cleans the caves
up for me?* That would be silly.

But he hated the idea of getting
filthy. He would never usually sign
up for anything that meant he would
trash his clothes or look stupid.

"I guess..." he said glumly.

"That's the right spirit, Harry,"
Bear said cheerfully. "You might not
get a choice about having to be a
survivor, but you always get a choice
about how you think about it. If you
can think positively then your body
finds it a whole lot easier to follow."

Bear pulled another oversuit out
of his rucksack. It was like the one
he was wearing, but it was blue, and
crisp and brand new. It looked fresh
off the peg.

Harry breathed a sigh of relief.
Maybe he could get away with not
getting too messed up.

"You can wear this over what
you've already got on," Bear said.
"It's tough and rugged. Some of

the rocks in there are sharp, and wet skin swells and damages very easily, which means you could pick up cuts and bruises that will get infected. This will protect you."

"So – it's not going to keep me dry?" Harry checked.

"Sorry, champ. Nothing will keep you dry down here. But at least the suit can keep you a bit safer when you do get wet."

While Harry pulled the oversuit on,
Bear pulled out another helmet, and
a pair of scuffed, well-used boots.

"These are vital too. Your head
needs protection, and the boots will
give you a grip on wet surfaces, as
well as proper ankle support."

Harry was tempted to sniff the
boots first and make sure they were
clean inside, but Bear was looking.
He laced them up while Bear took
his white trainers and stowed them
in his rucksack.

Harry looked at the helmet. It was really going to mess his hair up. But before he could say anything Bear had placed it on his head.

Bear began adjusting the straps so that it was a perfect fit. Like Bear's helmet, it had an LED lamp fixed to the front of it, and a chin strap to hold it in place.

"All ready to go?" Bear asked.

"I suppose." Harry decided not to say anything about the helmet then. He'd take it off later.

They turned their lamps on, and Bear led the way into the darkness.

4

LIMESTONE LABYRINTH

Bear and Harry sloshed through
shallow water that was flowing back
the way they had come. The deeper
they went into the passage, the
quicker the daylight faded.

Their head torches were bright and
lit up the yellowy brown rock that
glistened with damp. As long as he
looked straight ahead at the area

37

the torch, lit up, Harry found that
he could see perfectly. Either side
of the bright beam, however, there
was nothing but darkness.

The further they walked, the more
Harry thought about the walls of
the passage. They were covered in
smooth bumps, like the roof of your
mouth. Harry shuddered. It was like
being swallowed by a giant throat.

If Harry had thought the air outside
the cave was hot, in here it was
hotter. The further they went, the
warmer the air became. Soon, it felt
like warm, wet blankets being stuffed
into his mouth.

"It's boiling!" Harry said.

"And humid too," Bear replied,
ahead of him. "There's a lot of
moisture in the air, which means
our sweat can't evaporate, so we
don't cool down. But we're still
losing water. So we'll be stopping
for regular water breaks."

Harry looked down at the stream.

"At least there's plenty of water
here!"

"There certainly is!" Bear agreed.
"These caves wouldn't be here
without it. There are hundreds of
miles of caves and tunnels down here,
all of them eroded by water over
hundreds of thousands of years."

"So why did the caves just stop

back at the cenote?" Harry asked.
"There was only one way in or out."

"Only one way in and out for us,"
Bear pointed out, "but the water can
go its own way."

"Ah-h-h." It dawned on Harry.
"So there might be more caves
underwater, right?"

"Got it in one. Some caves you
can only explore with air tanks and
wetsuits – but let's keep that for
another day, shall we?"

The tunnel soon began to shrink.
Bear had to duck to a half-crouch,
half-crawl. Salty sweat trickled down
Harry's forehead and ran into his eyes.
It was gross and it stung. He blinked,

hard. He could feel his hair plastered to his head. Yuck. Harry undid his helmet strap and took it off, and the light from his headlamp swung all around the tunnel.

Bear immediately said, "Woah!"

"I'm just sorting my hair," Harry explained. "The helmet's so hot and it's squashing my hair down."

"That's fine, but we don't move until your helmet is back on," Bear said. "You don't realise how hard your head can hit solid rock. Just a normal walking pace could mean a nasty crack and a head wound."

Bear sounded serious. Harry could tell he wouldn't budge until he put

the helmet back on. He slicked
his hair back, out of his eyes, and
put his helmet back on again. He
thoughtlessly stood up straight –
and immediately his head hit the
rock ceiling with a dull 'clonk'.

"Woah!"

Bear grinned.

"You see what I mean, buddy?"

Harry did. Okay, the helmet didn't look good but at least it was keeping him from injuring himself. Even with the helmet on it had really hurt to bang his head against the rock. He crouched down like Bear as they moved forward.

After a few minutes they reached a junction where the tunnel split in two directions. The stream flowed out of the right-hand tunnel. Bear's lamp lit up a small pile of stones by the left-hand one.

"This way," Bear said, heading to the left. The new tunnel sloped upwards a little, out of the stream. The walls were still damp, though.

By now, Harry had learnt that the walls were always damp.

Harry looked at the pile of stones as he clambered past it.

"Did you put those stones there?" he asked.

"Yes, I used them to mark my route on the way down," Bear said. "Your markers stand out if they're obviously man-made, like a pyramid of stones or the shape of an arrow. Anyone who sees them will know they've been put there for a reason."

The tunnel got larger again. They could move more easily, but they still weren't exactly walking. Everywhere they went, they had to climb and scramble and pick their way carefully. There wasn't a single smooth surface anywhere.

You could tell that this place had been carved out by nature, Harry thought. Humans hadn't had a hand in it.

Soon the tunnel widened into a larger cavern. The ceiling looked like it was covered with thousands of stone needles. Some were just a few centimetres long, some were a couple of metres. The floor was the same, with stone needles sticking up.

"Stalactites!" Harry said, looking up at the ceiling. He moved his head and ran his lamp over the floor.

"And stalagmites. Dad taught me a trick to remember which is which. When we hang the washing out at home, my mum's *tights* hang down, like stalactites do."

He knew that both the stalactites and stalagmites were formed by the build-up of tiny particles of calcium found in the water that dripped from the roof of the cave.

"Good one," Bear smiled. "Right, there are a whole lot of tunnels leading off this place but our way out's over here. Mind your step, it's going to be uneven."

They picked their way through the mass of stalagmites to another crack in the far wall. It was narrower than the one they had come in through and at its tallest point was only as high as Bear's waist.

Bear went first, almost having to lie on his front to get into it.

Harry crouched down and watched Bear disappear. After about a minute he saw Bear stand up in a black, empty space.

Bear called back to him. "Your turn!"

Harry found it easier than Bear had, because he was smaller. But whenever he lifted his head to see where he was going, his helmet clonked against the rock again. His lamp reflected straight back into his eyes from the rock in front of him.

When his chest pressed into the rock, Harry could feel the dampness soaking in to his oversuit. He tried not to think what he looked like now.

Then Harry felt space opening
up around him. He could stand up
straight. The dampness had soaked
through the oversuit and he could
feel his T-shirt clinging to his chest.
He was covered in dirt.

"We can take a breather here,"
Bear said. "We've earned it."

The air was full of the sound of
rushing water, but Harry couldn't see
what was causing it. That small little

crack had brought them into a cavern
that had to be ten metres in all
directions.

Harry dragged his attention away
from his grimy clothes, and moved
his head around and up and down,
to sweep the lamp beam around.

He looked up, and the circle of light
fell onto a falling torrent of water.

A waterfall! It disappeared into
a hole in the ground.

And next to the cascading water
was something so ordinary it looked
completely out of place.

A rope. It hung next to the fall and
disappeared up into the dark.

"Is that the way out?" Harry asked warily.

"That's right," Bear said. "Straight up that fall."

5

WATER OBSTACLE

Bear gave the rope a tug to check it.

"This got me down, and it'll get us up again. Are you any good at climbing?"

"Sure," Harry said truthfully. "I've been on the climbing wall loads."

The wall at Camp was one of his favourite activities. He loved the challenge of stretching out his hands and feet between the rubber grips and footholds. It was indoors so he could wear his best stuff whilst he showed off his skills. He really felt he was achieving something, pushing his body up against gravity, and he knew he looked good doing it.

"That's good news, Harry," said Bear. "Can you handle a slope like this?"

"Um – sure. I think."

Harry felt fairly confident. The slope wasn't completely vertical, just very steep. He guessed he could manage it. But the climbing wall at Camp was clean and dry. It didn't have a waterfall tumbling down next to it.

"Take this. It's proper caving rope," Bear said, passing it to Harry to have a feel. "It's flexible and designed to shed water, so we can still get a grip on it. Try it."

Harry gave it a pull.

"Uh-huh," he said politely.

Bear had been right that you could get a good grip on it. But it was covered with droplets of water from the waterfall's spray, and all that water went somewhere.

Specifically, it trickled wetly over his fingers and wrists and down his sleeves. He couldn't wipe his hands without getting more dirty.

But at least he knew they had
the right equipment.

They had a quick break, drinking
some water from Bear's bottle and
each eating a ration bar. Then Harry
was first up the rope.

Hundreds of tons of water roared
by in the opposite direction. He made
sure his boots were firmly planted
with each step and hauled himself
up the rope, hand over hand.

Pretty soon his arms were aching from all the effort. The fall drenched him in spray, but his oversuit protected him.

Eventually Harry climbed over the ledge at the top, where Bear had tied the rope to a stalagmite.

"I'm up!" he called, and settled back to wait for Bear. He rolled up his sleeves to cool himself down, and looked down at his oversuit. It was damp, but the sturdy material wasn't soaked through. *Neat piece of design,* Harry thought approvingly.

The rope went rigid as Bear climbed up. While Harry waited, he flashed his lamp along the tunnel ahead. It was the first time that Harry was in the lead since they had entered the caves. Beyond his light, there was nothing but pitch darkness. Just mile after mile of caves, he guessed.

The tunnel was narrow and twisty, so he would have to be careful where he put his feet. And they would be sharing it with the stream that was flowing rapidly downhill towards the waterfall.

"Why does everything bend so much?" he wondered as Bear clambered up to meet him. "Why doesn't the water wash the stone away in straight lines?"

"Great question! It's all limestone, but it's not all the same strength," Bear said as he reached the top.

"Limestone is made from the remains of marine animals, like coral or shellfish. Over millions and millions of years their bodies leave calcium behind."

Bear untied the knot in the rope as he spoke. "So limestone doesn't go in straight lines because living creatures don't go in straight lines. There might be other bits mixed up in it, or air bubbles trapped in it. The water just follows the lines of weakness."

Bear coiled the rope up and put it in his rucksack.

Together they set off again up the tunnel, picking their way over rocks and trying to stay out of the stream.

Soon they came to another of Bear's little marker piles. This one was below a hole in the ceiling that was about two metres above them.

"Up we go," Bear said.

He gave Harry a boost up to the next level, then climbed up behind. Harry tried to stand up, but his helmet clonked against the roof again. He had to squat. In fact, he had to lie almost on his front to go any further.

This bit wasn't much more than a crack.

"We'll have to go leopard-style for a while," Bear said. "But don't worry, it gets bigger. I'll lead."

Bear took his rucksack off and pushed it ahead of him. Then he slowly disappeared like a snake going into a hole, pulling himself along on his elbows. Harry watched the soles of Bear's boots get further away.

A couple of minutes later it was Harry's turn.

The crack really was narrow. Harry had pulled his sleeves back down again but he could feel his elbows grinding into the limestone through the fabric.

For the first time, Harry started thinking about the millions of tons of rock above him. If even just a few rocks came down he could be blocked in here forever ...

He told himself not to be stupid. Bear had done this. He could too.

But it was a huge relief when he popped out into a larger chamber and could stand up again. Beyond the lamp light, the chamber turned into a new tunnel, continuing onwards.

Bear grinned and handed Harry another ration bar and his water bottle.

"I think we've earned a top-up!"

Harry took a long drink. "What happens if we run out of water?" he asked.

"Well, this water around us has been filtered by miles of limestone," Bear said. "So it should be clean to drink if we need to."

Harry looked around at the glistening walls, and down at his clothes. Nothing looked clean.

"So, where did all this dirt come from then?"

"Most of it's limescale – dissolved calcium left behind by the water. Some of it will be silt left over from when the cave was flooded." Bear took a sip from the water bottle.

"Water coming straight out of the rock will be absolutely pure," Bear explained. "But there's always a risk that algae growing in the damp might contaminate it, so we'd need to be careful how we collected the water. We'll drink from our own supplies for as long as we can."

Something caught Harry's eye right next to him in a pool. A little pile of rocks was sticking up out of the water.

"Why did you put a marker underwater?" Harry asked.

"I didn't," Bear said, frowning. "I put them all where I could see them."

Bear took a long hard look at the pile, then back at the crack they had come through.

"Wait here," he said, before disappearing.

A couple of minutes later he returned. His face was thoughtful.

"There must be a rainstorm on the surface, and it's all coming down here. The water's almost up to the ceiling back the way we came. And that pool there is the tunnel I came through the

first time. It must have flooded from the other side."

Bear looked serious. "It's not rainy season yet, but a survivor always has to expect the unexpected, Harry."

"The water's rising!" Harry gasped.

Bear nodded.

Harry's heart thudded. He thought again of those millions of tons of rock between him and the open air. With water plugging up the only exits they had.

"You mean ... we're trapped?"

6

HARRY'S CAVERN

"Not quite," Bear said immediately.
"If water's coming in, that means air
is getting out. Otherwise air pressure
would hold the water back. So, if
the air can find a way out then so
can we."

Harry peered up the tunnel ahead
of them.

"You said you got here through this pool – so, you haven't been up the tunnel that way?" he asked.

"I haven't."

Harry felt excitement swell in his chest.

"So, we might be the first humans who see what's up there? That is cool."

Bear grinned.

"You've got the explorer's spirit, Harry!"

Together they set off into the new, unexplored caves.

It took more walking, and climbing, and scrambling. At a junction of three passages, they made another marker pile and took the middle passage, because it was slightly bigger than the others. They still needed to crawl.

The passage narrowed abruptly into an even smaller crack. About a metre and a half in, there was a lip of rock. Harry couldn't see beyond it. It would be a tight squeeze to get around it.

"Okay," Bear said thoughtfully. "I really need to know what's round that corner. If the tunnel stays this narrow, I won't be able to get any further."

"I could have a look?" Harry suggested. He was smaller than Bear. "You can pull me back if I get stuck."

"Okay," Bear agreed. "Take care and don't go too far in."

Harry crouched down with his heart pounding, and pushed himself into the crack.

To move forward, he had to lie on his side with his hands in front of him and wriggle like a caterpillar. If the crack stayed this narrow then Bear would definitely get stuck, and that would be it.

Harry reached the lip of stone, and pulled himself around it. He squeezed his head and shoulders out, and felt empty air all around him.

Harry grinned, and was about to pull himself out of the crack when he realised he hadn't checked what was below him. He quickly glanced down. Phew. The floor was only about a metre down.

Harry called back.

"It's okay. There's plenty of room here."

He waited while Bear pulled himself through, looking around at the new cavern. The first ever human to see it!

It was the biggest yet, and the most spectacular. It was higher than a house, and the size of several rooms all knocked together. The walls and floor and ceiling were covered in forests of stalagmites and stalactites, and strange, natural sculptures like melted statues.

Harry found himself staring at something like a spider's web that was made of stone.

Bear emerged next to him, and whistled as he looked around.

"We'll call this one Harry's Cavern! Okay, let's take a break first, and then we'll look for the way out."

They sat on a ridge of rock and ate a couple more ration bars.

Harry felt he had to ask. "What happens when we run out of bars?"

"We'll find food," Bear told him. Suddenly, he reached up to the rocky wall behind Harry. He was holding a ... thing. Harry flinched away from it.

It was like a spider, but with even more legs, wide enough to take up all of Bear's palm. The front pair of legs ended in claws and they all grew out of a black, armoured body. A single, thin spike stuck up like a tail at its rear end.

"This little guy's a whip scorpion. He's not poisonous," Bear said, setting it down and watching it scuttle away into the shadows.

"And if you don't fancy eating him," Bear went on, "there were fish back in that cenote. We'll be okay."

"Now, Harry," Bear went on, "we'll find the exit quicker if we both look. I'll go round this way, you go round that way. As long as we can see each other's lights, we won't get lost."

Bear looked at Harry seriously. "Check the ground with every step you take, Harry. What looks like a shadow could be a hole, and you won't know how deep it is until you've fallen down it."

"We'd better make a pile by this hole," Harry pointed out. "They all look the same. We might end up going back the way we've come."

"You took the words out of my mouth!" Bear smiled.

Harry and Bear pulled some small, loose rocks into a small pile at the foot of the crack they had come out of. Then they split up to explore Harry's Cavern. Harry went clockwise.

Harry took great care where he was putting his feet. The amazing rock formations meant there wasn't a flat surface anywhere so he spent a lot of time looking down at his legs – and seeing just how filthy his oversuit had got.

But instead of feeling annoyed, he just smiled to himself. There were only two choices – get out of here, dirty, or stay here forever with nice, clean gear.

No contest. Even though this cavern

was amazing, the idea of seeing his friends and family again was better. He couldn't wait to get home to tell them all about it.

After every careful step, Harry moved his head to shine his lamp all over the walls and floor, and even up at the ceiling. There might be a hole up there, hidden by the small forest of stalactites.

In fact, he almost kept his eye on the ceiling too long. Harry took another step, looked down, and saw a crack yawning in front of him.

"Whoa!"

Harry quickly stepped back.

"Are you okay?" Bear called across the cavern. His light flashed into Harry's eyes. "Did you find something?"

"Uh – yeah, I'm fine," Harry called back.

He peered into the crack. It was about a metre deep, a metre long, half a metre wide. There was a thin layer of mud and gunge at the bottom. It was a dead end.

"And I haven't found anything yet," Harry added.

It was still the same when he met up with Bear five minutes later, on the other side of the cavern.

Bear bit his lip thoughtfully.

"There will be an exit. Remember, these caves were carved out by water. For millions of years, water was getting in and flowing out. It went out through the crack we came in. But where did it come in?"

Bear put his hands on his hips and looked around. His lamp flashed over all the nooks and crannies and shapes in the rock that they had explored.

Bear kept on thinking out loud.

"We've been going uphill for most
of the time. We must be getting close
to ground level. There could even be
a way out, so small we can't see it.
There's one thing we haven't tried,
though ..."

Bear reached up to his helmet
and switched his lamp off.

Then, before Harry could react,
Bear had switched off Harry's lamp,
too.

The whole cavern was plunged
into total blackness.

7

THROUGH THE U-BEND

"Do you see anything?" Bear asked
out of the darkness.

"I can't see a thing," Harry said.

There was literally *no* light. At all.
Anywhere. Not a glint or a glimmer.
Harry tried to think of the darkest
thing he had ever known. His room at
home, on a night with no moon, and

the curtains drawn, in the middle of a power cut. Nope, darker than that.

Coloured shapes floated in the back of his eyes, like they always did if someone turned the lights out back home. But even they faded away, and then there was nothing. The darkness was as solid as the rock all around them.

"Let's try something," Bear said. "Look away from my voice, and tell me if you still can't see anything."

Something very faint, pale white, moved in the corner of Harry's eye. He looked towards it and it vanished.

Harry looked away. And there it was again – in the corner of his eye.

"I *think* I can see something," he said. "Sort of. But not all the time."

"Right. Is it moving?" Bear asked.

The light moved slowly. Up. Then down.

"Uh – yes. Like it's bouncing."

"That's my watch." It was weird, but Harry thought he could hear a smile in Bear's voice. "That was just to show you how our eyes work. We are expert at picking up tiny little things in the corner of our vision."

Harry watched the light as Bear kept explaining. "It's a skill leftover from when our ancestors hunted on the plains. That tiny little movement might be a sabre-toothed tiger hiding in the grass. Nowadays it means we notice some things better if we don't look directly at them. Right. Are you facing my voice?"

"Uh-huh," Harry confirmed.

"I'm holding my arms out towards you. You do the same."

In the dark, they took hold of each other's elbows.

"And now," Bear said, "stare straight ahead, and we'll turn on the spot. Slowly. Clockwise. Okay, go."

They shuffled together in a slow

And Harry saw a light.

It was like Bear's watch – the tiniest little glimmer. But only if Harry wasn't looking right at it.

Harry's heart beat with excitement.

"I see something," he said.

"Right, point at it. Then close your eyes because I'm about to turn our lamps on."

"Okay. Pointing."

Harry shut his eyes. Through his eyelids, he sensed the lamps come on. He kept pointing as he opened his eyes slowly to let them adjust.

He was pointing at the crack he had nearly fallen into earlier.

Harry and Bear stood on either side of it and peered at the bottom, a metre down.

"I didn't think there was anything here," Harry said.

"Certainly looks like a dead end," Bear agreed. "But see how it bulges out a little at the bottom? It could be hiding a way out. If there's a way through under that ..."

Bear lay on his front and tried
to lower his top half down to peer
underneath the bulge. He tried several
times to get at the right angle.

Harry could see the problem. Bear
would almost have to stand on his
head, in a crack that was a metre
deep, and only a little bit wider than
Bear was. It would be very hard for
him to get back up out of it.

"I can do it," Harry suggested.
"I'm the right size, and if I get
stuck, you can pull me out."

Bear smiled.

"Okay, well volunteered, mate.
Let's do this."

Harry lay down on his front, then put his arms out and lowered himself vertically in. Bear held onto his feet. Harry's hands and the top of his helmet went into the sludge at the bottom of the crack. The years of slimy mud that lined the walls of the crack covered his oversuit. Harry ignored it all and peered, upside down, under the lip of rock.

Fresh air blew very gently onto his face, and light shone down on him. Natural, yellow daylight.

"There's a way out!" he called excitedly.

"Can you get to it?" Bear called down at him.

"Yeah ... I think so ..."

Harry was lying in one half of a U-shaped tube. If he could squeeze under the lip of rock then he would come up the other side.

But then Bear was pulling him back out again.

When Harry was back on his feet,

and had wiped his hands on his oversuit, which didn't make anything much cleaner, Bear asked, "Can I get to it?"

Harry had to think about that.

"Um. It's going to be tight but ... I think so, yes."

"Okay. Here's what we're going to do. I'll help you through. Then I'll push my stuff through, then I'll come myself."

Harry had a nightmare vision of Bear, wedged in the U-bend forever.

"Supposing you can't get through?" he asked.

"Sometimes you just have to take things as they come." Bear smiled. "Put it this way – I can't stay here, can I? Some things, you just don't worry about until you have to. Save your energy for later. If I get stuck ..." He smiled again. "Then you'll just have to go for help!"

And so Bear helped Harry down again. Harry wriggled forward at the bottom of the crack. Rock scraped roughly at his oversuit and sludge slimed itself onto the fabric. His helmet grated against the sides of the crack.

But now he had the fresh air and daylight to spur him on.

With a few more kicks and wriggles,

suddenly Harry was through on the other side.

"I'm through – I'm sure you can fit too!"

"On my way!" Bear called through the crack.

Harry clambered up and looked around.

And his hopes plummeted.

He was at one end of another tunnel that stretched away into the darkness. It was not as wide as Harry's Cavern, but taller. There weren't as many stalagmites or stalactites.

A beam of sunlight
shone down through a
hole in the ceiling, onto
a pile of crumbled rocks
and dead leaves and
vines. The hole was the
size of a manhole cover.
It was almost covered
with plant life, but
sun and air could get
through.

But the ceiling was
four metres above
Harry.

There was absolutely
no chance of climbing
up to it.

8

STONE STATUE

"Can you take my things, Harry?" Bear called.

First, Bear pushed his helmet through the crack.

"What about your head?" Harry called back, remembering how much it had hurt when he hit his own head.

"It's a calculated risk, Harry.
This is so narrow that I can't afford
anything that might get me stuck.
So I'll just have to be careful of
my head. Rucksack coming next."

Harry pulled the bag as soon as it
came through. And then he waited.
The sound of scrapes and scuffles
told him that Bear was squeezing
himself through the crack, but
there was no sign of him.

Harry crouched down, ready to
help Bear out. He waited some more.
The minutes felt like hours.

Finally, Bear's arms and head
appeared, followed by his shoulders
and then the rest of him.

"Whoo!" Bear exclaimed, once
he was finally standing up again.
He put his helmet back on. "I don't
want to do that again! So, what have
we got?"

"I don't think we can get out this
way," Harry said sadly, nodding at the
ceiling hole. He tried to be positive.
"But I guess there's a lot more tunnel
to go down."

Bear went and stood in the beam
of sunlight.

"I think you're right, Harry," he
agreed. He reached up and grabbed
one of the vines that dangled down
through the hole. It snapped and fell
down on top of him in a small flurry
of dirt and leaves.

"These are all too thin," Bear said thoughtfully. "We've still got the rope, but we don't have any way of getting up there to anchor it ... Woah!"

Suddenly the air was full of dark, fluttering, furry shapes blocking out the light. Instinctively, Harry and Bear both ducked. The creatures swarmed around the hole and then disappeared up it, like a reverse whirlpool.

"Wow!" Harry said, smiling. "Bats!"

He had studied them in a school
project. They were cool. The only
mammals that could fly.

Bear smiled too.

"This place is a natural shelter
for them. Looks like they're all gone.
I was about to say – no place to
anchor the rope, so we press on."

"At least we know we're near
the surface," Harry said. It was
a comforting thought, after the
disappointment of seeing sunlight
but not being able to get up to it.

"Absolutely. Give it a few more
centuries, and that roof might crumble
completely. This place will become
another cenote."

They were just about to start walking when Harry's eye fell on something in the pile of debris beneath the hole. Whatever this was caught his attention because it was obviously man-made. He bent to pick it up.

"Wow!"

It was a statue, the size of a small doll. It looked like a person, if people really looked like they did in the pictures Harry's little sister liked to draw. Arms and legs sticking straight out. Square head, full of teeth.

"Look at this, Bear!"

Bear took the statue gently, letting out a low whistle as he looked.

"Great spot, Harry!" he said. "The ancient peoples who used to live in this part of the world thought the caverns were entrances to the Underworld, so they would throw offerings in for their gods."

Bear turned the statue over in his hands. "Limestone's a soft rock so it's handy for carving. When you make a sacrifice then you offer nothing but the best, so whoever made this would have slaved over it for days, maybe weeks, to get it exactly right. This guy must be centuries old."

Bear handed it back.

"Cool!" said Harry. He was the first person to touch it in hundreds of years!

The statue wasn't very big. Harry thought it would make an amazing souvenir.

But then he thought of the person who had made it, like Bear had described. Taking it wouldn't be very respectful. So Harry carefully put the little figure back where he had found it, and picked up a pointy lump of limestone instead.

The lump was shaped a bit like
the end of a tooth, probably the tip
of a fallen stalactite. One day, Harry
decided, he would carve his own statue.

Then it was time to move on,
away from the beam of daylight.

At first they could walk normally,
but the tunnel soon began to get
lower and narrower. Bear went first,
and before long they were crawling
again.

A strange new smell was tickling
Harry's nose. Something sharp that
went straight to his tear ducts and
made his eyes water. It was like ...
toilet cleaner. At least, that was
what Harry's brain said it was, but
he knew it couldn't be.

"I've found where the bats live," Bear said without turning around.

"Yeah?" Harry said, interested. He tried to peer around Bear. "Where are they?"

"Well, there's none here at the moment," Bear said, "but that wasn't what I was warning you about." He sounded amused. "Look down."

Harry's lamp shone down on a black, sticky layer that covered the rock in front of him. That eye-watering smell was coming from the sticky stuff.

Harry realised what he was about to crawl through.

"Yeurch! Bat poo!"

Bear chuckled.

"The technical term is 'guano', and hey, it's one hundred per cent natural product! Just think of it as a lot of fruit and insects ... mashed up a bit. The smell is ammonia."

Harry pulled down his sleeves to cover his hands, and kept crawling. Then his helmet clonked against the ceiling. It was getting even lower. Up ahead, Bear was now crawling on his front.

"Oh, you're kidding me!" Harry groaned.

"You can do it, Harry!" said Bear. "You've already shown loads of courage today. This is just another great opportunity for you to choose to be brave."

Harry gritted his teeth, closed his eyes and lay down on his front. Slowly he dragged himself through the revolting gunge.

His eyes streamed and the fumes made him sneeze. Sneezing made it worse, because then he had to breathe in deeply. Meanwhile, the stinking, sticky mess clung to his oversuit.

Harry grimaced as something cold and wet dripped down his neck hole and down his back.

After some more twists and turns, the tunnel sloped up, and then suddenly they emerged into a larger cavern. Bear high-fived him.

Harry didn't bother looking down at his front. He could imagine the mess – and smell it. Instead he looked around for the next way out.

He turned a small circle, with his lamp flickering over the rocks.

"It's another dead end!" Harry sighed. He knew the drill. "Okay, so we turn our lights off ..."

"First things first, buddy," Bear reminded him. "We haven't explored yet!"

They set off in opposite directions. Harry and Bear each found a clue at the same time.

Harry found a piece of dead wood, as long as his arm.

Bear found a pool of water.

"How did this get here?" Harry asked. He held the wood. "It couldn't have come down that crack we came through. It would've got stuck."

"It came through here," Bear said thoughtfully. They shone their lamps into the pool. In the clear water they could see the start of a new tunnel. "It got washed through the last time this cave flooded. Hold on."

Bear reached over, and again switched off both their lamps.

This time they didn't have to try hard to see the light. It was right there in front of them.

At the other end of the flooded tunnel.

Bear turned their lamps on again and smiled at Harry.

"How long can you hold your breath, champ?" he asked.

9

BREATHE DEEP

Harry thought before he answered Bear's question. He couldn't take his eyes off the tunnel.

He was used to the caves by now. He knew how narrow passages could get as you crawled through them. It could be hard, even when you could breathe just fine.

But now he had to do it underwater. That was a whole new level of difficulty.

"Well," he said, trying to keep his voice calm, "I can swim a width of the swimming pool back at Camp, underwater."

"Brilliant!" said Bear. "That should be fine."

Bear started to get the rope out. "This time, though, I'm going first. It's best if I check out the way through, in case there's anything unexpected. You hold onto this end of the rope, and once I'm through, tie the rope around your waist and I'll pull you through after me. Easy!"

Bear looked confidently at Harry. "And if I get into difficulty, you'll be able to feel it on the rope and haul me back. Okay, Harry?"

Harry had been trying to control his worries, but the fear suddenly increased. "But what if I can't pull you out?"

Bear smiled. "It's okay. Remember, I'll be floating, so it'll be much easier than pulling me out of that crack would have been. And we managed that, didn't we? All along we've just dealt with what's in front of us, haven't we?"

Harry nodded.

"And that's all we're going to do

now. We don't need to worry. We just need to move carefully but swim confidently – just like you would underwater in a swimming pool."

"Okay," said Harry, managing a half smile.

"Now, we need to get ready for this. We need to breathe slow and deep, like this. In ... out ..."

Harry copied Bear. The swimming instructor at Camp had told him about breathing this way too. When you don't breathe, carbon dioxide builds up in your blood and makes you want to gasp for air.

Harry thought that would be awkward, halfway along a flooded tunnel. So the best thing to do if you were going to be underwater for a while was to get as much oxygen into your blood as possible in advance.

"That's it," Bear said. "Let your shoulders go up, stick your stomach out too, get your lungs as full as they can go."

They breathed together until Harry's head felt a bit fizzy and Bear decided they were both ready. Bear tied the rope around his waist.

"I'll give a single pull on the rope to say I'm through. Three pulls or more means I'm in trouble and you need to get me back," Bear said.

Harry nodded. Bear went on.

"Give one pull yourself when you're ready, and bring the rucksack through with you – I'll need my hands free to swim, but when I'm through I can haul you on the rope and you can pull it with you. Okay, Harry?"

Harry nodded again.

"See you on the other side, then!"

Bear took one last breath and dived under.

Harry was left alone. He'd not
noticed before, but it was so quiet
in the cave. He let the rope pay
out through his fingers as Bear
swam through the tunnel. All he
could hear was his own breathing.

How long would this take? A
minute? Two? How long could he
hold his breath?

Harry told himself to think about
more positive things. Like the fact
that the way out of these caves was
just a few metres away! He knew that
he'd be glad to see the last of them,
but he was also glad he had done it.

Harry looked down at himself.
Wow, he was totally filthy! Mud and
limescale and bat poo. He thought

of his clothes under the oversuit. They were probably ruined by now with grime that must have soaked through.

He grinned. For the first time ever, Harry didn't care what he looked like. So what? He had helped Bear get through the caves by being brave and working hard, not because of what style of outfit he was wearing.

The helmet and oversuit and boots weren't stylish, but they had protected him from knocks and scrapes. They were grimy and battered, but Harry wasn't. They had protected him. That was all that really mattered, Harry thought.

Just then, the rope twitched in his fingers, once.

Bear had made it!

Harry quickly tied the rope around his waist, took another few deep breaths, and eased into the cool water. He filled his lungs one last time, gave the rope a tug, gripped the rucksack to his chest and dived under.

The water roared and whooshed and gurgled in his ears. Almost immediately he felt himself moving forward as Bear pulled the rope in.

Harry bumped and scraped along the tunnel, the helmet taking most of the knocks.

And then he was out!

When Harry broke through the surface Bear was crouched on a rock. "Brilliant, Harry!" he said. "I'm really proud of you."

Harry just grinned and sucked clean air into his lungs.

Looking around, he could see that behind Bear was a short passage that sloped upwards like a tilted chimney. Behind it, at the far end, Harry could see sunlight.

When he'd finally got his breath back, he leaned back and shouted with glee.

"We made it!"

Bear laughed and cheered. "Yup! Just a short climb from here."

Bear helped Harry out of the water, and coiled the rope up around his shoulders. Bear led the way up the chimney on his hands and knees.

Harry crawled after him, out into sunlight. They were in a small hollow, a few metres deep, with steep sides. Tall jungle trees towered over them in every direction.

"One more little obstacle – no problem," Bear said.

He tied a loop in the end of the rope, and threw it up to lasso a boulder on the rim of the hollow. He tugged at it to check it was holding firm, then walked up the slope, pulling himself hand over hand. Bear grinned down at Harry.

"Now, you do the same, and we are well and truly out!"

"I'm coming!"

Before he grabbed the rope, Harry instinctively wiped his hands on his oversuit to clean them. After the wiping, they were even more filthy – covered with guano.

Harry smiled, cleaned his hands as best he could on the rocks and grabbed the rope. He went up the rock-face the same way Bear had done, gripping on to the rope as he powered up with his legs.

At the top, Bear reached out a hand but as Harry stretched towards it, his boots slipped. His feet shot backwards and he landed with a thump on his front.

"Hey, Harry! You okay?"

"Ow!" Harry laughed. "Yeah, I'm fine..."

He pushed himself up on his arms, stared at the ground, and stopped.

This wasn't the cave, or the jungle.

He was on a platform made out of wooden slats.

Harry's head whipped round.

The person talking wasn't Bear.

Harry was lying on the wooden platform on the adventure playground at Camp. No jungle. No hollow. No Bear. The Frisbee game on the football pitch had just come to the end of another quarter.

"Come on!" George urged. "It's our turn again!"

10

BETTER THAN BAT POO

There wasn't time for Harry to work
out what was going on.

The teams were running to take
their places and the ref was waiting
to begin.

Harry wasn't wearing a filthy caving
oversuit or a helmet that squashed
his hair. He was wearing his sports

kit and he still had the compass
zipped away in his shorts pocket.

His teammates were calling him.
Quickly, Harry raced after George
onto the pitch.

The ref checked her watch and
blew her whistle for the next quarter
to start. The Yellow team was ahead,
so the Reds took the first throw.

George was the first to catch the
Frisbee after throw-off. He chucked
it towards Harry, but it started to
curve away towards Lily, a girl on
the other team.

Harry ran hard after it, his feet
pounding on the grass.

"Aargh!" he bellowed as he reached Lily just before she caught it. She flinched and Harry snatched the Frisbee.

He passed it on, and it zigzagged down the pitch through two more players. Suddenly the Red team had scored to equalise.

But Harry couldn't celebrate the goal. He'd grabbed the Frisbee by scaring Lily away. He felt bad.

The game started up again and the Frisbee went back and forth and around the pitch. No one scored for several minutes and it was still a draw as the end of the quarter approached.

A girl on the Yellow team had the Frisbee. She had a choice of people to pass it to, all calling for it. Harry was marking one of them. Between her and Harry there was a big, wet patch of mud.

The Frisbee raced through the air towards the player Harry was marking.

Harry charged straight across the muddy patch, eyes on the Frisbee. He felt the mud splash up onto his socks and legs and shorts, but he didn't care. He leapt up and grabbed the Frisbee out of the air, landed and chucked it to George, all in one movement.

George flicked it into the goal, a moment before the ref blew to mark the end of the game, and a Red team victory.

"They thought you wouldn't run to catch it there," George laughed as they celebrated. "You're covered in mud now!"

Harry grinned. The rush and buzz of the Frisbee game had pushed the whole cave adventure to the back of his mind, but suddenly he was reminded of all the dirt and danger.

He couldn't explain it, but here he was. It had to have been some kind of weird dream, but even so, he knew that he had learned a lot from it.

"Well," Harry said, "it's better than being covered in bat poo!"

Now it was George's turn to look puzzled.

"Um – I guess."

Harry smiled. Then he noticed Lily, standing on her own, looking sad.

He felt bad again.

He hated people who threw their weight around to get what they wanted. And that had been exactly what he'd done when he'd frightened Lily and snatched the Frisbee.

Harry walked over to her.

"Hi, Lily. Listen ... um ... I'm sorry if I scared you back there. I really didn't mean to."

"It's okay," Lily said. "I know you didn't. It's hard to stand my ground sometimes."

"Right ..." Harry didn't really know what to make of that. "Still friends?"

"Oh ... yes." Lily smiled. "Still friends."

Harry felt a bit better.

As they left the field, Harry wished he could help Lily, to make up for scaring her. Then he felt the stupid compass with five directions in his pocket.

He pulled it out. It had just the usual four directions now – North, South, East, West. His mind really was doing strange things today.

Harry felt something else in his pocket, solid and heavy.

Frowning and puzzled, he took it out.

A piece of pale yellow rock. Limestone. Pointed, like the end of a tooth, but smooth. Perfect for carving a statue out of.

Harry stared at it.

How did that get there?

Somehow, this limestone rock had found its way back from his dream about the cave.

The cave was real! It *couldn't* have been a dream. So was everything that went with it. Bear and the adventure had been real – and he'd learned so much.

What did the compass and its five directions have to do with it all? Harry took it out and looked at it again. Was this what started it? Could it do it again?

Could the compass help Lily have an adventure and learn something too?

Harry looked up.

"Hey, Lily!"

Lily sighed.

"Harry. Look, it's really okay, I'm fine ..."

"No, it's not that," he assured her.

Harry held out the compass.

"I, um, thought you might like this?" he said. "Just consider it a gift."

The End

Bear Grylls got the taste for adventure at a young age from his father, a former Royal Marine. After school, Bear joined the Reserve SAS, then went on to become one of the youngest ever people to climb Mount Everest, just two years after breaking his back in three places during a parachute jump.

Amongst other adventures he has led expeditions to the Arctic and the Antarctic, crossed oceans and set world records in skydiving and paragliding.

Bear is also a bestselling author and the host of television programmes such as *Survival School* and *The Island*.

He has shared his survival skills with people all over the world, and has taken many famous movie stars and sports stars on adventures – and even President Barack Obama!

Bear Grylls is Chief Scout to the UK Scouting Association, encouraging young people to

have great adventures, follow
their dreams and to look after
their friends. Bear is also honorary
Colonel to the Royal Marine
Commandos.

When Bear's not travelling the
world, he lives with his wife and
three sons on a barge in London,
or on an island off the coast of
Wales.

Find out more at
www.beargrylls.com

This brilliant **Bear Grylls Adventure** is set in a reader-friendly font and design, for maximum enjoyment for everyone.

The font we have used is called OpenDyslexic. You can find out more about it here: **www.opendyslexic.org**

Dyslexia affects as many as 1 in 10 people, and often makes reading more difficult. We wanted to make our books as easy to enjoy as possible, so this special font and a design with lots of space helps us do just that.

Not everyone with difficulty reading has dyslexia, and not everyone with dyslexia has the same difficulties. You can find out more about dyslexia on these wonderful websites:

The Dyslexia Association: **dyslexia.uk.net**

British Dyslexia Association: **bdadyslexia.org.uk**

Dyslexia Scotland: **www.dyslexiascotland.org.uk**

Did You Know?

- Stalactites hang down from the roof of caves and stalagmites grow up from the floor of caves, formed by calcium that drips through the water. But there are also twisty shapes called helictites, which go in all directions from the ceilings, walls and floor.

- Lots of animals use caves for shelter, like bats, but some creatures never leave the deepest parts of the cave systems, and these are called troglobites. Snails, spiders, salamanders and aquatic animals such as shrimp and fish all live in caves and often will be blind or have no body colour.

- The world's largest cave is believed to be Son Doong in Vietnam's Phong Nha-Ke Bang National Park. It is estimated to be between two and five million years old and is more than three miles long, with caverns big enough to house skyscrapers and the world's tallest stalagmite.

- Cave exploring – sometimes called pot-holing, caving or spelunking – is a popular thing to do, but it can be dangerous. In June 2018, a football team in Thailand got trapped in the Tham Luang Nang Non caves for more than two weeks by rising floodwater. Thanks to expert divers in a heroic rescue, all 13 people were eventually brought out alive. Unfortunately, one Thai diver, Saman Gunan, lost his life delivering oxygen tanks and a statue is now erected at the caves to his memory.

- The British Cave Rescue Council (BRBC) is a voluntary charity which works with the emergency services in Great Britain and internationally. Some of their members were the experts called to the Thai Tham Luang caves. If you ever need them, dial 999!

Find out more at **www.caverescue.org.uk**

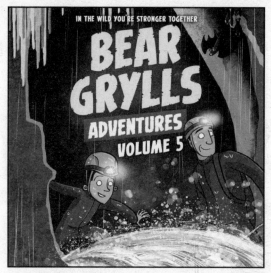

Cave Challenge & Mountain Challenge

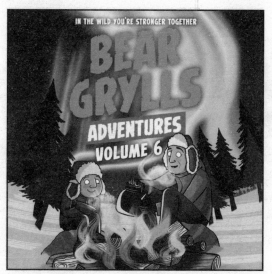

Arctic Challenge & Sailing Challenge

 Available at all audiobook retailers

THE BEAR GRYLLS

FOR MORE INFORMATION ON
BEAR GRYLLS, CHECK OUT

beargrylls.com

ADVENTURES SERIES